Hopeless

We carried the trays of snacks down the hall to Stephanie's room. As soon as we closed the door behind us, Kate said to Patti, "You haven't told us — did you talk your parents out of moving to Alaska?"

Patti frowned unhappily. "No — I just *couldn't* say anything. They're so excited about all the advantages for Horace and me — "

"What advantages?" I wanted to know.

"Oh, like incredibly clean air, and wide open spaces — " Patti began.

Stephanie, Kate, and I looked hopelessly at one another.

"Let's eat before the food gets cold," Kate said brightly, changing the subject.

But I don't think anyone was hungry. I'm usually starving, and even I had no appetite at all. Were we really losing a Sleepover Friend?

Look for these and other books
in the Sleepover Friends Series:

No More Sleepovers, Patti?

Susan Saunders

AN
APPLE
PAPERBACK

SCHOLASTIC INC.
New York Toronto London Auckland Sydney

ISBN 0-590-41696-0

12 11 10 9 8 7 6 5 4 3 2 1   8 9/8 0 1 2 3/9

Printed in the U.S.A.   11

First Scholastic printing, December 1988

Chapter 1

"I wonder what Patti's dad wanted to talk to her about?" said Stephanie Green. We were coasting downhill on our bikes toward Riverhurst Elementary School.

Kate Beekman backpedaled and looked thoughtful. "It's not her grades, that's for sure. Patti Jenkins is one of the smartest kids in the whole fifth grade."

"And I can't really see Patti in any kind of trouble," I added.

I think I know Patti pretty well by now. I'm Lauren Hunter. Not only do Stephanie, Kate, Patti, and I ride our bikes together to school and back practically every day, we do just about *everything* together.

It wasn't always the four of us, or even the three of us. In the beginning, it was just Kate and me.

Kate and I are almost next-door neighbors on Pine Street — there's just one house between us. We started playing together while we were still in diapers, and by the time we got to kindergarten we were best friends. That's when the sleepovers started: Every Friday night, either Kate would sleep over at my house, or I'd sleep over at hers. We'd make Kool Pops in the freezer and s'mores in the microwave, and call it "cooking." We'd play school or grown-ups, dressing in our moms' clothes and shoes. Sometimes we'd spend a whole night making up silly ghost stories.

The Sleepover Twins, Kate's dad named us. Actually, we're nothing alike — Kate's small and blonde, I'm tall and brown-haired. Kate's neat, and I'm messy. She's very sensible, and I let my imagination run away with me sometimes. So Kate pulls me together, and I like to think I loosen her up a little. In our case, opposites make great friends.

My brother Roger always said Kate and Stephanie didn't get along at first because they were too much alike: "Both bossy!" Stephanie moved into a house at the other end of Pine Street the summer before fourth grade. She and I sat next to each other in 4A, Mr. Civello's class.

Stephanie told neat stories about the stuff she'd done back in the city, which is where she lived before

Riverhurst. She was funny, she knew tons about dressing and the latest styles, and she was a great dancer. After I'd known her for a couple of months, I asked her to a sleepover.

I guess Kate had a certain way of doing things, and Stephanie had another way. Anyhow, they didn't exactly see eye-to-eye. Kate thought Stephanie was a big show-off, and Stephanie thought Kate could be a real party-pooper. Still, a few weeks later, Stephanie invited the two of us to a sleepover at her house. Then she came to my house again . . . and finally Kate and Stephanie became used to each other.

Last September, Patti Jenkins turned up in Mrs. Mead's fifth-grade class, along with Kate, Stephanie, and me. Although you'd never guess, Patti's from the city, too. She and Stephanie even went to the same school in kindergarten and first grade, but the two of them are totally different. Patti is as quiet and shy as Stephanie is talkative and outgoing. And she doesn't like cities at all.

Stephanie wanted Patti to be part of our gang. Four girls would make it even, she told us. Kate and I liked Patti right away — there isn't anyone nicer. It wasn't long before there were *four* Sleepover Friends.

Not that Friday morning, though. Patti had phoned Stephanie earlier. "I just wanted to let you know that I won't be meeting you at Pine Street," she said.

"Are you okay?" Stephanie asked, because she thought Patti sounded kind of funny.

"I'm f-fine." Patti stammers when she's upset. "Dad has something he wants to s-speak to me about. H-he'll drop me off at s-school."

"She said to wait for her at the bike rack," Stephanie told us.

"It feels kind of weird with just the three of us, doesn't it?" I said to Kate and Stephanie as we stopped at the traffic light.

Kate nodded. "Like the old days."

Stephanie grinned. "I notice you didn't say the *good* old days."

Kate, Stephanie, and I pedaled up to the curb in front of the school. Patti wasn't at the bike rack, so we tried to spot her in the crowd of kids streaming up the walk.

"I don't see her anywhere," Kate said.

Suddenly somebody burped really loudly, right in my ear!

"Ick! You are *so* gross, Wayne Miller!" I growled.

4

Wayne's this hulk in 5A who thinks it's cool to be as rude as he can.

"You better have a motor in that piece of junk," Wayne said, giving my bike a thump. "Or Ronny and I are going to blow you girls totally off the road!"

Wayne was talking about the Chamber of Commerce Twenty-Mile Bike-a-thon around Riverhurst a week from Saturday. It wasn't really a race; for each person who actually finished, the Riverhurst Store-Owners Association was going to contribute a certain amount of money to the parks fund. Wayne and his friend Ronny Wallace had bumped into Patti and me going over part of the course, and they'd been teasing us ever since.

"Girls in an endurance contest — give me a break!" Wayne snickered.

"Oh, yeah? Patti and I could ride to the state line and back with one leg tied to the handlebars!" I told him.

Wayne just made another rude noise and strolled toward the front steps of the school.

"Lauren, you're so competitive!" Kate raised an eyebrow. "I thought the Bike-a-thon was supposed to be *fun*."

"He really makes me mad," I muttered. "And you're pretty competitive yourself, Kate Beekman!

What about your tape for the video club? You stuck with it because you wanted to make a video better than the sixth-graders', didn't you?''

"I'm only competitive about things that matter, and I couldn't care less about Wayne Miller," Kate sniffed.

"Stephanie, what a great jacket! I always love your clothes." Christy Soames, a girl in 5C, Mr. Patterson's class had come up behind us. She's one of the best-dressed kids at school.

Stephanie was wearing her stone-washed, dark-red denim jacket with a black-and-white plaid lining. Red, black, and white is Stephanie's favorite color combination — it goes really well with her dark curly hair. "Thanks, Christy," Stephanie said. "I picked it up at a little boutique in my old neighborhood, back in the city."

Kate sighed loudly. I didn't know if it was directed at Stephanie, because Kate was afraid she'd start going on about the city again, or at Christy, because Kate thought she was a total air-head. It didn't really matter, since neither of them paid a bit of attention.

"Isn't shopping in the city fabulous?" Christy squealed. "It makes the stuff around here look like *garbage*."

Where did that leave Kate and me? I wondered. Neither of us owns a single item of clothing from anyplace other than the Riverhurst stores. Even when we went to the city to spend the weekend with Stephanie's grandmother, all I bought was a ball for my kitten. Kate didn't buy anything.

"The city's where I found these suede boots," Christy went on, barely pausing for breath. "I was walking down Logan Lane with my mom, and they practically jumped out of a store window at me."

Actually, they were nice-looking boots, reddish-brown with tops that folded down just above the ankles, but Kate made an unmistakable gagging sound.

"I couldn't say no to them — they were *so* perfect — and then I just had to get this belt to go with them." Christy showed Stephanie her reddish-brown belt with silver conches on it, but not Kate and me. We obviously weren't in their league, stylewise.

"Which store?" Stephanie asked, really getting into it.

"Canfield's, across the street from Gems 'n' Stones, the big jewelry store," Christy said. "My mom had just stopped into Gems 'n' Stones to buy a ring, two kinds of gold with a green — "

"If we have to listen to one more word of this,"

7

Kate was muttering to me through gritted teeth, "I'll stuff her green, one-hundred-percent pure silk scarf in her mouth." Much louder, Kate added, "It's almost time for the bell," which interrupted the shopping lecture.

Christy looked down at her brand-new green plastic watch with the yellow face. "Oh, you're right! See you, Stephanie." She nodded at Kate and me and hurried across the lawn.

"Christy Soames is truly incredible!" Kate said, exasperated. "Do you realize she can't talk about anything other than shopping?"

"Well, *you* talk about movies a lot," Stephanie said.

"Shopping is not a career!" Kate snapped. She would like to be a movie director some day — she loves movies. Horror movies, musicals, old movies, new ones, foreign films, silents, you name it, Kate'll watch it.

"Listen, maybe Patti's inside," I said, cutting off Kate's reply. It really was getting close to the bell. "You know how Patti hates to be late."

But Patti's desk at the back of the room was empty. She didn't show up until five minutes after the bell had rung, with a note for Mrs. Mead. And her eyes were puffy.

"I think she's been crying!" Stephanie whispered over her shoulder to Kate and me, since we sit right behind her.

"Quiet, please," said Mrs. Mead, shaking her head at us. "Class, take out your math homework. Stephanie, go to the board and show us how you got the answer to problem one."

It wasn't until lunchtime that we got the answer to why Patti seemed so upset. We didn't want to pounce on her in the hallway. But as soon as we sat down at our usual table in the cafeteria, Stephanie, who's always direct, asked, "Patti, are you in some kind of trouble?"

Patti shook her head and looked even more unhappy. "I'm not in trouble at all. My dad wanted to tell me about these great new jobs he and my mom might be offered."

"What great new jobs? What's wrong with their old ones?" Stephanie asked. Patti's parents are both history professors at the university in Riverhurst.

"Where?" Kate asked, before Patti could answer. I knew Kate was trying to get right to the point of the problem.

"Back in the city?" I guessed, because that's where the Jenkinses taught before.

9

"No, at a college in . . . in *Alaska*," Patti mumbled, her lower lip twitching.

"*Alaska!*" Stephanie, Kate, and I exclaimed at the same time.

"Anchorage," Patti said. Her eyes welled up. "Can you believe it?"

Visiting Patti in the city wouldn't have been much of a trip for us, but Alaska! I don't think you could get any farther away from Riverhurst and still be in the United States!

Patti went on, "Tomorrow we're driving to the airport, getting on a plane — "

"All of you are going?" Stephanie asked.

"Yes. Mom, Dad, Horace, and I." Horace is Patti's little brother, named after some ancient Roman who lived two thousand years ago. "We're flying to Seattle," Patti said. "Then we'll catch another plane to Anchorage. Mom and Dad will go to the university for interviews, and after that we'll sightsee — check things out, I guess."

"There was a program on TV about Alaska last month," Kate said. "Beautiful snow-covered mountains, and lots of animals: moose, black bears, elk, foxes. . . ."

"Sure, it would be a great place to visit, but I

don't want to *live* there!" Patti wailed. "I like Riverhurst!"

"Maybe things won't work out," I said soothingly.

"Yeah — maybe your parents won't get the jobs after all," Stephanie added hopefully.

"I can't count on it," Patti said. "The university there wanted them to come so badly that they're paying for all the plane tickets, our hotel, and everything!"

"How many days will you be gone?" Kate asked her.

"Ten," Patti said. "I'll be out of school all next week. I'll miss the science fair!"

The Riverhurst Elementary School Science Fair was the next Wednesday afternoon. Kate and Stephanie and I hadn't entered it, but Patti had. "Adelaide has worked so hard to learn her tricks," she added.

Adelaide is Patti's kitten, a sister to my Rocky, Stephanie's Cinders, and Kate's Fredericka. And she was Patti's science fair entry, "The Truth About Cats." The tricks were to prove that cats *aren't* stupid, the way some people say they are.

"We've got a party to do tomorrow afternoon,

too," said Kate. The four of us have a birthday party business for little kids: Patti and I dress up like clowns and entertain the guests, while Kate and Stephanie videotape the whole thing. Sometimes it seems as though we'll have to do parties for the rest of our lives, just to make our monthly payments for the video camera Stephanie ordered for us on an impulse! Most of the time it's a lot of fun, but when a dozen little kids get rowdy or cranky, it really takes all four of us to handle them.

"Oh, wow — I completely forgot about the party!" Patti groaned.

"And the Bike-a-thon next Saturday?" I added.

Not only had Patti and I spent time going over the course, we'd been doing workouts together after school for the last month or so, building our legs up for the race.

You know, exercises like holding onto the back of a chair with both hands, rising up on our tiptoes, then bending our knees and squatting down slowly, staying on our toes the whole time. We also did leg lifts lying on our stomachs, and about a million scissor-kicks. We were really ready for it! Only now there wouldn't be any race, because it wouldn't be fun doing it by myself.

"Oh, Lauren, I'm sorry!" Patti wiped her eyes with a napkin. "This is awful!"

"You'll talk your parents out of it," Stephanie said firmly. She's an only child, and she can talk her parents out of — or into — almost anything.

Patti shook her head hopelessly. "I'm not very good at that. . . ."

"Cry if you need to," Stephanie advised.

Kate frowned at Stephanie. She doesn't really approve of some of Stephanie's methods. "Don't worry, Patti," Kate said. "The four of us will come up with something at the sleepover tonight."

"You can still come, can't you?" I asked.

Patti sniffled and tried to lighten up. "Yes, I can come. Our plane doesn't leave until one, and I promise you, I won't wreck the party by crying all night."

"Patti!" Stephanie, Kate, and I said in unison. It was just like her to be worried about spoiling our fun when she was being whisked off the next day almost up to the North Pole.

"It'll be our best sleepover ever," Stephanie said. "To give you something to remember when — "

Kate poked her under the table.

"Ouch!" Stephanie complained. Patti didn't even notice. She had bigger things on her mind.

13

"Oh — there's something I'd like to ask you guys," she said then. "Horace is leaving his snake and lizard collection at school for the kids in his class to take care of. I guess I could board Adelaide at the Riverhurst Veterinary Hospital, but I thought she'd be a lot happier if one of you could take her."

"I'd love to keep her, but I don't know how she'd take to Bullwinkle," I said. Bullwinkle is our dog — Roger's dog, really, since Roger picked him out at the animal shelter when Bullwinkle was a tiny puppy. The people at the shelter said Bullwinkle was mostly cocker spaniel, pointing out his floppy ears and thick, black fur.

As soon as we got him to our house, though, he started to grow. He passed cocker spaniel size in two months, Labrador in four. By the time Bullwinkle was a year old, my parents had figured out he was mostly Newfoundland, if not grizzly bear. He weighs around a hundred and thirty pounds, and he's over five feet tall when he stands up on his hind legs. "*You* know Bullwinkle wouldn't hurt a fly," I said to Patti, "but Adelaide might not think so. Remember, Rocky hid in my laundry hamper for the first month I had him."

"I don't have Bullwinkle, but I do have Melissa," Kate said gloomily. Melissa the Monster is Kate's younger sister. "And she takes a lot of getting used

14

to. Fredericka always hisses when she sees Melissa coming. Besides, my mom is always saying, 'One pet's the limit in this household.' "

"It's no problem for me, Patti," said Stephanie. "No humongous dog, and no little sister, either. Plus, my mom is wild about cats. Cinders will be glad to have the company."

"That's great!" Patti said, smiling for the first time that day.

"Why don't you bring her over tonight?" Stephanie suggested. "That way, you can help her get settled."

"I'll show you what she's learned," Patti said.

"Right — maybe she'll encourage Cinders to do something besides eat and sleep!" said Stephanie.

"Hey, what if we bring Fredericka and Rocky, too?" Kate said with a grin. "Kind of a family reunion!"

All of us giggled.

"That's a terrific idea!" said Stephanie. "I'll get all their favorite snacks: sardines, tunafish. . . ."

"Rocky likes cheese," I said.

"And Fredericka loves shrimp dip," Kate added.

"It's the beginning of a new club!" Stephanie said.

"The Sleepover Kittens!" said Patti, laughing.

15

Chapter
2

On our bike ride home that afternoon, Stephanie and Kate and I planned the sleepover. (Since Patti was so late that morning, her father had dropped her off. Her mother picked her up after school, too.) "I think I'll ask my mom to drive me to Charlie's," Stephanie said, "so I can buy stuff for ice cream sodas and floats."

Charlie's Soda Fountain is on Main Street. Each of us has our own favorite drink there, made with Charlie's famous homemade ice cream. Kate's is a Coke float, with two scoops of creamy vanilla. Stephanie always orders a fudge ripple chocolate milkshake. I like the banana smoothies, made with incredible banana ice cream churned up in a blender. And Patti's drink is a pale-green lime sherbet freeze.

"What about food?" I asked Stephanie. "Want us to bring anything?"

"I'll make my fudge," Kate volunteered. It's a super-fudge, really, with double the amount of chocolate, plus tons of marshmallow fluff. "I'll bring some brownies, too — Patti really likes brownies."

"And I'll do my specialty — onion-soup-olives-bacon-bits-and-sour cream dip," I said.

"My dad's going to pick up a pizza," Stephanie said, "so that should take care of the munchies."

"There's a great horror movie on at nine," Kate said. *"Island of the Undead."*

"I hate horror movies!" I protested.

"Oh, Lauren, this is a classic!" Kate argued.

"Patti hates them, too," I reminded her. "And she's not exactly feeling strong."

"So no *Island of the Undead*," Stephanie said a little wistfully. She thinks horror movies are *funny*. "What do you think Patti would like to do?"

"She likes to play Mad Libs," said Kate.

"I thought of a great one the other day — " Stephanie began.

She was interrupted by two boys who whizzed past us on bikes. "Where are your training wheels, girls?" they shouted.

"Wayne Miller!" I muttered. "And Ronny."

17

"Ignore them," Kate said to me. "They're so immature."

"Just wait till they find out Patti and I aren't going to be in the Bike-a-thon after all. I'll never hear the end of it!" I said.

But Stephanie and Kate were still thinking about Mad Libs. " — using the Beauty Column from *Teen Topics*," Stephanie went on, "but leaving out some of the major words, like 'My hair is very blank, but all my friends say it's because I blank too often. How can I put more blank in my blank?' "

"Or, 'I just can't seem to find the right blank for my blank. Does anyone make a blank for a blank like me?' " Kate giggled, and I did, too.

"Excellent!" said Stephanie as we turned into Pine Street. "Think of some more before tonight, okay? And don't forget the cats, and the food!"

"I can't believe it was just this morning that I was saying how weird it felt without Patti. . . ." I sighed. "I guess we'd better get used to the feeling."

"No way. I refuse to accept that she's going *anywhere*," said Stephanie. "Either Patti will talk Mr. and Mrs. Jenkins out of the whole thing, or . . . or they'll get to Alaska and decide that they hate it! Her parents aren't exactly outdoorsy, are they?"

18

Kate and I grinned. "Not exactly."

Patti's mom and dad had lived all of their lives in big cities until they moved to Riverhurst. Mrs. Jenkins probably didn't know the difference between regular ivy and poison ivy. And Mr. Jenkins's idea of outdoor fun so far seemed to be sitting in a lawn chair on the patio and reading a history book.

"All Alaska is . . . is outdoors!" Stephanie said, making her point. "See you at six-thirty. Dad should get home with the pizza about then."

Kate walked over to my house at six-fifteen. Roger was going to drive us to Stephanie's on his way to pick up Linda, his girlfriend, but we had plenty of time to kill. Anybody who thinks it takes girls a long time to get ready for a date ought to check out Roger on a Friday evening.

Kate and I dragged out the atlas and looked up Anchorage. "Well, at least it's in the *bottom* of Alaska," Kate said.

"Still, if one inch on this map equals two-hundred-fifty miles . . . ," I said.

Kate measured with her fingers. ". . . and it's more than thirteen inches away. . . ."

I quickly multiplied 13 times 250, math being

one of my better subjects. "It's more than three thousand two hundred and fifty miles away. And that's in a perfectly straight line!"

"Lauren!" Roger shouted from the hall. "You and Kate come on, or I'm going to be late!" As if it were our fault. Brothers!

Kate and I climbed into the backseat of Roger's old car with our usual backpacks, a cardboard box with Fredericka in it, three shopping bags full of food, and Rocky, wrapped in a little blanket. He can't stand to be closed up in a box.

Roger dropped us off at Stephanie's house at the end of Pine Street, and we struggled up the sidewalk. Stephanie came out to help. "Let's put the kittens in my room," she said, taking the box Kate was carrying. "Patti got here just this minute — she's letting Adelaide get reacquainted with her brother."

"Are you sure 'reacquainted' is the right word?" Kate said as we followed Stephanie down the hall — from behind the closed door of Stephanie's room came a couple of blood-curdling yowls and some hisses that made Rocky's hair stand up!

Stephanie set Fredericka's box on the floor and threw open the door. Her kitten, Cinders, was standing in the middle of the bedroom, his tail puffed up to twice its normal size, his back arched like a Halloween cat's.

Cinders is coal-black — Stephanie would never have had a kitten who clashed with her bedroom, which is decorated in red, black, and white, of course. Patti's kitten, Adelaide, is black with a white chest and white feet, like Rocky. Adelaide was huddled on the top of Stephanie's bookcase, glaring down at her brother and yowling like a cougar.

Patti was scrambling around, picking up the floor lamp and the books that Adelaide had knocked down when she headed for higher ground. "I'm really sorry, Stephanie," Patti said. She added worriedly, "They don't seem to be getting along very well."

"As soon as they settle down — " Stephanie began, when Rocky suddenly squirmed out of my arms. He landed with a thud on Stephanie's black-and-white rug. The blanket was still wrapped around him, but Rocky untangled himself like a magician and leaped on Cinders's back with a fierce growl!

Fredericka heard the noise and sprang out of her cardboard prison like a jack-in-the-box. She jumped into the fight with all four orange paws. Adelaide bailed out of the bookcase not two seconds later, joining the large, wriggling ball of black, white, and orange fur that was rolling around the floor!

"Rocky, stop that!" I shouted.

"Fredericka, I'm ashamed of you!" Kate yelled.

"Cinders!" Stephanie grabbed the nearest cat's tail, and got a scratch on her arm.

"What in the world is going on in here?" Mrs. Green peered around the bedroom door, took one look at the fighting kittens, and disappeared into Stephanie's bathroom. She was back in a flash with a glass of water and a towel.

"This ought to do it. . . ." Mrs. Green dumped the water onto the wrestlers.

There were four howls of protest. The mound of kittens exploded: Adelaide ended up on the bookcase again, Rocky scooted under the desk, Fredericka skulked behind the closet door, and Cinders scrambled onto a bed, complaining loudly. All four of them started licking their wet fur disgustedly.

Mrs. Green handed Stephanie the towel to wipe up the floor. "I think you'd better separate the kittens before they pounce on each other again," she advised. "Then come to the kitchen — your dad is here with the pizza, Stephanie."

"Mom's probably right. Separate 'em, at least

while we're out of the room," Stephanie said. "Let's see . . . we'll leave Adelaide here, since she has to get used to staying in my bedroom. Kate, why don't you put Fredericka in the bathroom for now, and Rocky can have the spare bedroom. Cinders will wander around the rest of the house."

We divided up the cats. Apart from one another, the three visitors calmly began to explore their new territory. Then we hurried to the kitchen with our shopping bags of food. Mrs. Green helped us stack two trays with plates, glasses, ice, a king-size Dr Pepper, slices of Tony's pizza with extra cheese, my special dip, and a bag of potato chips.

"We'll get the desserts after we've finished this," Stephanie decided. "Shakes and freezes from Charlie's will go better with brownies than with nachos and pizza, don't you think? The kittens will have to wait for their grub, too."

We carried the trays down the hall to Stephanie's room. As soon as we closed the door behind us, Kate said to Patti, "You haven't told us — did you talk your parents out of Alaska?"

Patti frowned unhappily. "No — I just *couldn't* say anything. They're so excited about all the advantages for Horace and me — "

"What advantages?" I wanted to know.

"Oh, like incredibly clean air, and wide open spaces — " Patti began.

"We didn't think your parents even liked the outdoors!" Stephanie interrupted.

"Are you kidding? Before my parents had Horace and me, they went camping almost every weekend!" Patti told her. "For their honeymoon they hiked through the wilderness, alone, for two weeks!"

"Oh, great!" I moaned. "Secret explorers!"

Stephanie, Kate, and I looked hopelessly at one another. "So if that won't work . . ." Stephanie said.

"I'm afraid nothing will work," said Patti. "These jobs would mean promotions for both of them, and a whole lot more money, too."

Stephanie nodded — the very reasons her father had left the city for Riverhurst. "There's probably nowhere to spend extra money in Alaska," she said gloomily. "What could you buy? A new harness for your dogsled team?"

"Let's eat the pizza before it gets cold and the cheese turns to rubber," Kate said brightly, changing the subject.

But I don't think anyone was hungry. I'm usually starving, and even I had no appetite at all. Were we really losing a Sleepover Friend?

24

Chapter
3

The kittens certainly hadn't lost *their* appe-
tites — all that wrestling had made them as hungry
as tigers. Stephanie served them a great dinner:
Shrimp dip as an appetizer, little slivers of soft
cheese, chopped sardines, and a big spoonful of
tunafish. We put one bowl in each of the four corners
of Stephanie's bedroom — as long as the kittens were
chowing down, they certainly weren't going to get
into a fight — and placed each of them in front of a
different bowl.

Patti's kitten was first to lick her dish clean. The
other kittens seemed pretty content, so when Adelaide had finished washing up, Stephanie asked,
"Can we see her tricks?"

Patti nodded. "Poor Adelaide thought she was

25

going to be a star, but I guess this is the largest audience she'll have." She picked up the kitten and set her down on Stephanie's desk. Adelaide just sat there, with a pretty dumb expression on her face. Her eyes were half-closed. This cat was going to do tricks?

"She looks like she's staring into space, with nothing at all on her mind, right?" Patti said. "Actually, she's checking things out. When cats aren't focused on anything right in front of them, their eyes shift to the sides to check out what's going on there."

Patti had done lots of reading for her science project, and she'd learned some interesting stuff. "Also," she went on, "if something moves up or down, cats can't see it well." Patti dropped a small piece of pizza crust straight down, right past Adelaide's nose. The kitten didn't even twitch!

"But if it moves *across*" — Patti sailed the crust past Adelaide sideways, and the kitten knocked it out of the air with her paws — "they lock in on it right away."

"Neat!" said Stephanie.

"If you pull gently on a cat's whiskers, its eyes will always close," Patti told us. Adelaide's eyes shut as soon as Patti touched her long, black whiskers.

"Why is that?" I asked.

"At night, when a cat is prowling around in the dark, it uses its whiskers like feelers," Patti explained. "As soon as the whiskers brush against a bush or a stump or something, it closes its eyes to protect them."

"Okay, Adelaide," she said in a high voice, because cats like high voices. "Up!"

Adelaide's eyes slowly focused on Patti's face.

"Up!" Patti said again. Adelaide raised up, balanced on her hind legs, and waved her front paws in the air!

"Wow!" I said.

"How did you teach her to do that?" Kate asked, amazed. "I can't even get Fredericka to move so I can make up my bed!"

"I worked with her a little bit every day. It just took a lot of patience, and" — Patti grinned — "food bribes. Then, when I saw how much she was learning, I decided it would be fun to surprise you all. Adelaide, roll over."

The black-and-white kitten rolled over three times, from one end of Stephanie's desk to the other!

"She already knows more tricks than Bullwinkle, and he's been around for eleven years!" I exclaimed.

On command, Adelaide sat up again. She spun around and jumped into Patti's arms from four feet away!

"I can't believe it!" Stephanie said. "I really didn't think you could teach cats anything, except maybe to come when you call them — if they happen to feel like it."

"There's a man in Florida with a trained house-cat act," Patti told us. "They stand up on their hind legs, bow, roll over, run an obstacle course — even jump through burning hoops. He says all you have to do is to get them while they're still young enough to learn, and you can teach them lots of things."

"Hmmm . . . maybe I can teach Rocky to clean up my room!" I said. My kitten had finished licking his face and was dozing off next to his food bowl. Fredericka was curled up on the rug, and Cinders was snoring on Stephanie's pillow.

"Cats have to have around nineteen hours of sleep a day," Patti said.

"No problem there," said Stephanie, plopping down on the bed next to her kitten.

"It's rotten that you're missing the science fair," Kate said to Patti, scratching Adelaide behind the ears.

"Maybe you could ask your parents to let you

stay with one of us, so you won't *have* to miss it," I suggested.

"No, I'd better find out what I'm getting into in Alaska," Patti said gloomily. She gave the kitten a squeeze before putting her down on the desk.

"Let's play Mad Libs!" Stephanie said, determined to be cheerful.

We played for a while, but every time Patti's turn came, she filled in the blanks with words like "ice cube," or "frozen," or "faraway." It didn't take anybody's mind off of Alaska.

"How about Trivial Pursuit?" Stephanie suggested.

"Great idea!" Kate said, a little too enthusiastically. Mrs. Mead sometimes lets us play Trivial Pursuit on Friday afternoon after a hard week, and Kate usually isn't happy about it. History and geography are not her strong subjects. But I knew what she was thinking: Patti is the smartest girl in the fifth grade. She always wins at Trivial Pursuit. Even though she's not the competitive type, the game was bound to make her feel better.

After Stephanie got it, we set up the board, chose our markers, and rolled the die to see who would go first. Stephanie won the roll, and we went clockwise from her to Kate to me to Patti.

Stephanie shook the die, blew on it, talked to it, and when the rest of us groaned, she finally tossed it daintily. She moved her marker (red, of course) to a green space. Green is for geography. Kate asked the question.

"What is the highest peak in the United States?"

Stephanie's mouth formed a thoughtful pucker. "Ummmm . . . Pike's Peak?"

Kate flipped the card to check the answer. "Sorry, Stephanie. It's Mount McKinley." The three of us nodded our heads together when we heard the answer; it was straight out of our fourth-grade science book.

"Oh, right," Stephanie said with a little shrug. Kate picked up the die. Then we noticed that Patti looked almost sick.

"What's wrong, Patti?" I thought maybe the pizza-shrimp-dip-sardine aroma in the room was getting to her.

Stephanie scrunched her forehead. "Where *is* Mount McKinley?" she asked.

Patti looked even more miserable.

"ALASKA," the four of us groaned in unison.

"Let's stay away from green," I suggested. Everyone nodded.

Kate rolled next and landed on yellow — history. Patti read the question this time.

"What was the forty-ninth state to join the United States of America?"

Kate smiled as if she knew the answer right away. She opened her mouth to speak. Then her eyes went really wide, and she snapped her mouth shut again.

"Well?" Stephanie said.

"Ummm . . . Hawaii?" Kate guessed feebly.

Stephanie and I looked at Patti questioningly. She didn't even need to turn the card over to check the answer.

"Thanks, Kate," she said. "Nice try."

By now, we all knew the real answer, but I flipped the card just to be positive.

"Alaska," I read glumly. I couldn't believe it. It must have been an omen.

For a couple of minutes, no one knew what to say. Kate and Stephanie like to make fun of me for being superstitious, but this time it really seemed as if someone were telling us that this was the beginning of the end for the Sleepover Friends.

In the quiet room, my stomach rumbled loudly.

"Lau-ren!" Kate said.

"At a time like this!" Stephanie said.

"I can't help it!" I protested.

Patti grinned. We all looked at her. "Actually," she said, beginning to laugh, "I'm a little hungry, too."

"You are?" Stephanie said. "To tell the truth, I could eat a little something myself." She got up to go to the kitchen, and we all followed.

"Ssh!" Stephanie cautioned as we tiptoed through the hall.

We whipped up our favorite drinks from Charlie's, grabbed some super fudge, and served up a plateful of brownies. Then we headed back into Stephanie's room.

"I think there's a two-hour 'Dancing Fools' on tonight," Stephanie said, turning on her TV. "Maybe we can pick up some new moves."

While she was changing channels, though, she flipped past a nature program. Two brown baby bears were tumbling around in a field of wildflowers and bright-green grass.

"Stop!" I yelled at Stephanie. "Let's just watch this for a second."

"Lauren . . . ," Kate said under her breath.

"They're so cute!" I murmured, ignoring her.

"You are such an animal freak, Lauren!" said Stephanie, but then she added, "Aren't they darling? They look like living, breathing teddy bears!"

Kate reached for the dial, but Stephanie covered it with her hand. "No, wait! There's the mother bear."

Kate tried to turn the sound down, but it was too late. "Alaska," said the announcer, "is our largest state. It's also one of our emptiest."

"Alaska?" I whispered.

"It's a rerun of the special I saw last month!" Kate growled.

"Almost half the state's entire population lives in Anchorage, which has most of the urban problems common to cities in the forty-eight continental states — "

Stephanie switched the television off, but not before Patti had gotten an earful. She dropped a half-eaten brownie back on the plate and looked sick. "Urban problems?" she said.

"Maybe that's good!" said Stephanie. "Your parents are trying to do the best thing for you and Horace, and they won't like the idea of — "

"You wouldn't necessarily be living right in Anchorage, anyway," Kate was saying at the same time.

"The mountains aren't that far away. . . ."

Were we supposed to be talking Patti *into* Alaska, or *out* of it?

The truth was that it didn't make much difference what we thought about Alaska. It was all up to Patti's mom and dad. I thought it would be a good idea to get as far away from that subject as possible, at least for the night.

"So — who's going to be the second clown tomorrow?" I asked Kate and Stephanie.

"I'm terrible at telling jokes," Kate said, making an embarrassed face. She was probably right. She doesn't exactly have a light touch. "I'll stick to videotaping the party."

"It's only a bunch of six-year-olds," Stephanie pointed out.

"I'd be a total disaster," Kate said firmly.

"Then I guess it's up to you, Stephanie," I said.

"Do we really need two clowns?" Stephanie said cagily. "Maybe this once we could manage with one."

"What am I supposed to do? Ask the joke questions and answer them, too?" I replied. I was getting a little cross.

Patti and I call ourselves Sparkly and Barkly, and our costumes are pretty simple. We use those colored

34

zinc-oxide sunblocks to paint ourselves up. Patti draws big yellow stars with red tails on her cheeks. Then she spreads glittery silver eyeshadow on the rest of her face — Sparkly, right? Plus, she's made antennae out of a plastic headband, pipe cleaners, and Styrofoam balls.

As Barkly, I tie my hair up in two ponytail dog-ears, paint my face in black, yellow, and brown splotches like a dog's spots, and wear a ratty fake-fur jacket of my mom's. I also hook a bike horn to my belt, so I can toot it a lot. Little kids really go for noise.

Sparkly and Barkly jump around, turn cart-wheels, and stand on their heads. They also ask each other dumb riddles. Sparkly: "What did the rug say to the floor?" Barkly: "Don't move! I've got you covered!" Then I toot my horn and howl. It's pretty silly and it's not the kind of entertainment I'd want at *my* birthday party, but first-graders love it. And we can make as much as thirty dollars for two or three hours of acting goofy, especially if we film the party with our video camera.

Stephanie was staring at herself in the mirror. "I look awful in yellow," she said.

"What are you talking about?" Kate said.

"The stars Patti paints on her cheeks — they're

yellow!'' Stephanie complained. ''They'll clash with any of my red, white, and black clothes.''

''So paint yours red and white,'' I said. ''What's more important is, how are your cartwheels?'' Patti and I are both pretty good at tumbling, but Stephanie and Kate aren't as into sports as we are. I'd never even seen Stephanie stand on her head.

''My cartwheels are just fine,'' Stephanie said huffily. ''I took gymnastics for a while in the city, for your information.''

''Good,'' I said. ''Then all we have to worry about is the jokes.''

''What's the theme tomorrow?'' Kate asked.

''Western,'' Patti answered. ''Mrs. Soames is having a cake in the shape of a cowboy hat, and plastic horses for favors.''

''It's at the Soameses' house?'' asked Stephanie. ''I hope Christy won't be hanging around.'' I could tell Stephanie was worried about acting nerdy in front of her.

''She'll probably be busy planning her next shopping spree in the city,'' Kate said disgustedly. ''Forget about Christy — focus on the jokes.''

''We'll do western stuff,'' I went on, ''like Why did the cowboy take his saddle and spurs to bed with him?''

36

"Easy, pardner. Because he was getting ready for nightmares!" Stephanie said. "Yuk, yuk! I have one. Knock knock."

"Who's there?" I said.

"You," said Stephanie.

"You who?" I said.

"Yoohoo! Ride 'em, cowboy!" Stephanie shrieked, cracking all of us up, and waking up the kittens.

"You'll manage fine without me," Patti said a little sadly.

Did she ever turn out to be wrong!

Chapter
4

Patti's mother came to pick her up in the middle of Mrs. Green's pancake breakfast. We all waved good-bye from the front door.

"Don't worry about Adelaide," Stephanie said.

"She'll be fine," said Kate.

Adelaide and Cinders did seem to be getting used to each other. When we woke up that morning we had found them both sleeping on Stephanie's desk, curled around each other on her quilted photo album.

"Don't worry about anything," I added.

"There's nothing left to worry about," Patti blurted out. "The worst thing that could possibly happen is already happening!" She dashed down the sidewalk, climbed into her mom's car, and rode away.

After Kate and Stephanie and I had put our plates in the dishwasher, I said, "Where's the Ouija? I want to ask it about Patti."

"Oh, Lauren — this is *serious*!" Kate groaned.

But Stephanie pulled it out of the closet in the front hall for me, and set it up on the kitchen table. Stephanie doesn't really believe in the Ouija, either, but she does think it's an interesting game.

A Ouija board is rectangle-shaped with a *yes* printed in the upper left corner, and a *no* printed in the upper right. The letters of the alphabet run across the center of the board in two lines that curve. At the bottom are the numbers *1 2 3 4 5 6 7 8 9 0*.

You set a little heart-shaped stand on top of the board, and you rest your fingers lightly on the edge of the stand. Then you ask the Ouija a question, and concentrate really hard.

In a few seconds, the stand will start to slide across the board, to point to "yes," "no," a letter, or a number. If everything is going right, the stand will actually spell out the answer to your question! I know, I know — there's probably no such thing as magic! But no one can really explain why the Ouija works the way it does. . . .

Stephanie and I put our fingers on the stand. "Kate?" I called.

"No way," Kate said, pushing her chair back. "I'm going to check on the kittens."

"She doesn't have the right attitude, anyway," I murmured. "Is Patti going to move to Alaska?" I asked the Ouija. I closed my eyes to concentrate as hard as I could.

At first, nothing happened. Then Stephanie said, "I think it's moving. . . ."

I opened my eyes to see the stand slide slowly across the board. It looked as though it was going to stop at the *D*, then on the *T*, but it kept on moving. The stand finally came to rest with its tip pointing straight to the *0* at the bottom of the board.

"Zero!" I said. "It's never done that before. Maybe we're not concentrating hard enough. Let's try again."

We set the pointer in the middle of the board and started over, but it ended up in exactly the same place, pointing at the zero.

"What's wrong with it?" I was asking as Kate walked back into the kitchen.

Kate looked down at the pointer. "Nothing," she said. "Patti knows zero about what's going to happen, we know zero, and the Ouija knows zero!

For the first time, I believe this contraption!" She added, "Lauren, my mom just stopped out front — we'd better get the kittens packed up."

"One more time?" I said, putting my fingers back on the pointer.

"Lauren . . ." Kate said sternly.

"All *right!* At least the Ouija didn't answer, 'Yes, Patti *is* moving!' " I followed Kate and Stephanie down the hall to the bedroom. Adelaide was lying on Stephanie's desk, her front paws tucked under her chest.

"You don't want to live in Alaska, do you, Adelaide?" I said to the kitten. She yawned, stretched, and blinked her big green eyes at me.

"Up, Adelaide," I commanded, not really thinking she'd pay any attention at all.

But Adelaide sat right up, balanced on her hind legs, and waved her little white paws in the air!

"Wow!" I said. "Adelaide, roll over!"

The kitten rolled over three times, just like she had for Patti!

"Jump, Adelaide!" said Kate.

Adelaide gathered herself together and sprang into Kate's arms!

"Listen," I said excitedly to Kate and Stephanie, "I have a great idea! Why don't we enter Adelaide in the elementary school science fair *for* Patti?''

"Yeah! Even if she doesn't win anything, at least all of her training hasn't gone for nothing," Stephanie agreed.

"We'll have a few days to practice with Adelaide before the fair, to let her get used to working with us," Kate said.

"I'll write down all the stuff Patti told us about cats," I said, "neatly, on a poster."

"Can you remember it all?" Kate raised an eyebrow. She was skeptical.

"Let's see . . ." I tried to recall what Patti had said. "When cats look unfocused, they're really studying everything around them."

"Right!" Kate said. "And they don't see anything very well if it's moving up and down, but they see great if something moves back and forth in front of them. And they close their eyes when you pull their whiskers — "

"And you *can* train a cat just as long as you start when it's still young enough to learn!" I finished.

"Let's do it!" Kate said.

Mrs. Beekman honked the horn a couple of times from the curb out front.

"Here's Rocky." Kate lifted him out from under a chair. I wrapped Rocky up in his blanket while Kate

42

put Fredericka in the cardboard box. We grabbed our backpacks and hurried to the front door.

"What time is the party at the Soameses'?" Stephanie asked.

"Two o'clock. My dad'll drive us over," I told her. "We'll pick you up around one forty-five, okay?"

"I'll be ready. See you then!" Stephanie called as we headed for Mrs. Beekman's car.

Chapter
5

Lunch was over, and I was almost finished painting my face when the telephone rang at my house.

"Lauren!" Roger shouted from downstairs. "It's for you!"

"Who is it?" I called back, not wanting to stop what I was doing.

"Stephanie!" Roger yelled. "She says she 'absolutely *has*' to speak to you — it's urgent!"

Urgent? Uh-oh. Stephanie was supposed to meet me in a few minutes — in her clown costume. I had a sneaking suspicion that Stephanie urgently wanted to get out of clowning and that she had come up with a scheme to do it. I rushed out of the bathroom and picked up the wall phone in the hall. "Hello?" I said.

44

"Hi, Lauren," Stephanie said. "I'm . . . uh . . . I'm afraid there's a little problem. . . ."

"What problem?" I said suspiciously. "Stephanie, you'd better not be chickening out — not this close to the party!"

"No, it's not that — not exactly, anyway," Stephanie said. Her voice sounded a little weak, especially for Stephanie. "I've sprained my ankle, Lauren. You know, the one I sprained at your house that time with Bullwinkle?"

"Oh, no, Stephanie. How did you manage to do that?" I groaned.

"I was practicing a few cartwheels in the backyard," Stephanie said sheepishly, "just to brush up. I really was planning to go through with it, and I wanted to look good. I guess I landed wrong."

"How bad is your ankle?" I asked her.

"It's not sprained nearly as badly as last time," Stephanie said quickly. "I can handle the Soameses' party, as long as I stay off my foot. I'll do the taping."

"We'd better hang up. I have to go over to Kate's and tell her she's a clown for the afternoon," I said. I was not looking forward to it one bit.

"Sorry," said Stephanie. "Kate's not going to be happy."

"It's not your fault," I said.

That's not what Kate said when I told her, though.

"Oh, sure!" Kate grumbled. "I'll bet you five bucks Stephanie just didn't want to look silly in front of Christy Soames!"

Patti hadn't been gone for more than a few hours, and it looked as though Kate and Stephanie already were starting up. Was it back to the old days without Patti around to smooth things over?

"Stephanie wouldn't do that," I said. "And we don't have time to argue about it, either, because we have to get your makeup on."

"My makeup!" Kate squawked.

"That's right. Mrs. Soames ordered two clowns, and Stephanie has to tape the party. I've brought over all the sunblocks, and an extra set of antennae. Put on whatever you're going to wear," I directed, "because if you put it on after you're made up, you'll smear everything."

Kate sat, scowling, on a chair in her room while I drew stars on her cheeks and filled in the rest of her face with glittery eyeshadow. She didn't say a word, just sighed angrily now and then. When I was finished, I set the antennae on her head and stepped back.

"You look really cute," I exclaimed, pleased with my work.

"What do you mean, 'cute'?"

"Well, Patti is awfully tall for a fairy," I explained. I added the last spots to my own face with the yellow sunblock. "I mean, Tinkerbell wasn't exactly a giant, was she? You're closer to the right size, the silver eyeshadow goes great with your hair, and the T-shirt is perfect." Kate had put on a long, pale-green T-shirt with yellow stars on it, and white tights.

"So I make a great-looking clown," Kate said. "Big deal." But she did stand up to peer at herself in the full-length mirror.

That's when her little sister, Melissa, bounced into the room, and I thought we were in serious trouble. You never know what's going to pop out of Melissa's mouth. If she said anything rude, Kate might back out of the party altogether.

"Wow! You look neat!" Melissa said to her sister.

Kate was so surprised that it took her a while to yell, "Melissa — will you *please* get out of my room!"

"Mom sent me to tell you it's one-thirty, and you'd better hurry up!" Melissa announced. She stuck out her tongue at us and flounced away.

"We can go over some jokes in the car," I said as Kate and I dashed downstairs and out the back

47

door. I have a couple of old joke books that belonged to Roger when he was a little kid. They're corny, but most jokes for five- and six-year-olds are corny.

We practiced a few jokes on the way over to the Greens'. Dad beeped for Stephanie, and in a few seconds she started down the walk, carrying the video camera.

"Look what she's wearing!" Kate exclaimed.

Stephanie had on a flashy red, black, and white sweatshirt we'd never seen before, a big, diamond-shaped rhinestone pin, and her black stretch pants. Her dark curly hair was pulled back on both sides with clips.

"Dressed to the teeth!" Kate muttered, staring down at her own clown outfit. "And she's barely limping!"

"Did you want her in a body cast?" I said.

"That's not what I meant, and you know it!" Kate hissed.

Stephanie wasn't limping very much, although her left ankle was bandaged.

"How's your foot?" I asked her as she slid into the backseat with Kate and me.

"Not too bad," Stephanie answered. "If I'm careful, it'll be fine by Monday."

"Or maybe even by tonight," Kate murmured.

"Just exactly what are you getting at, Kate Beekman?" Stephanie said.

"It strikes me as kind of funny that you just *happened* to sprain your ankle seconds before you were supposed to — " Kate began.

"Girls, *please* . . . ," cautioned my father from behind the wheel. "It's a beautiful Saturday afternoon, and all's right with the world."

Kate and Stephanie were quiet the rest of the way to the Soameses' house, just glaring at each other from time to time.

Mrs. Soames was waiting for us on the sidewalk. "Thank goodness," she said as soon as we'd gotten out of the car. "I was afraid you'd be late. Let's go in this way."

She led us around the back of the house, so that we could hide in the kitchen. Little kids were laughing and yelling in the front of the house.

"I haven't told Jeffrey you'd be here," Mrs. Soames said in a low voice — Jeffrey was the birthday boy, and Christy's little brother. When she saw Stephanie limping, Mrs. Soames exclaimed, "You've hurt your ankle! Why don't you sit down and put your foot up on this stool?"

Kate rolled her eyes at me as Mrs. Soames got Stephanie comfortable.

49

"Hi! I didn't know you guys were already here!" It was Christy, dressed to kill in gray wool baggy pants, pink suspenders, and a pink-and-gray striped sweater. Everything looked like she'd never worn it before, which she probably hadn't.

"Sssh!" Mrs. Soames put her finger to her lips, because Christy was shrieking, as usual. She has a really loud voice.

"Sorry!" Even when Christy is whispering, your eardrums tingle. She glanced at Kate and me. "How sweet," she said, writing us off with a word. Then she turned to Stephanie. "Stephanie, that's a terrific sweatshirt! Did you get it in the city, too?"

"Actually," Stephanie said, "my dad brought it to me from San Francisco. He was out there on a business trip, and he happened to be staying in a hotel right next to this little boutique. . . ." They were off and running.

"First I'll carry in the cake," Mrs. Soames was telling Kate and me. "When I say 'Happy birthday, Jeffrey,' you can pop through the door into the dining room. After you're done performing, we'll open presents and cut the cake."

Mrs. Soames showed us the cowboy-hat cake. It was iced in vanilla frosting with chocolate trim and had six candles stuck around the brim. Then she carefully backed through the swinging door with it.

"Do you like this color?" Christy was shrieking to Stephanie behind us. "Pink Perfection. My mom won't let me wear nail polish to school, but on weekends. . . ."

"Blah, blah, blah!" Kate said to me. "I can barely hear myself, much less Mrs. Soames!"

"Stephanie, you'd better get the camera ready," I warned. "It's almost time."

"Wow — do you really know how to use that thing?" Christy shrilled. "I'm impressed!"

"Quiet!" Kate hissed over her shoulder.

"All right, children," Mrs. Soames called out. "Please come to the table."

There were shouts of "Look at the cake!" "Can we eat now?" "Where's the ice-cream?" "Stop shoving, Danny!", and the sound of chairs being scraped across the floor.

Then Mrs. Soames gave our signal: "Happy Birthday, Jeffrey!"

"We're on!" I said to Kate.

Chapter 6

Sparkly and Barkly skipped into the Soameses' dining room, antennae bobbing and dog ears flopping.

"Clowns!" the kids all yelled and clapped their hands.

"Sparkly and Barkly!" shouted Jessica Freedman. She's our friend Mark's little sister, and we'd done a party at her house. Some of the others who had seen us before called out hello.

"How many bad guys can you put in an empty jail?" I screeched at the kids.

"Six!" Jeffrey Soames yelled.

"Twenty!" said Jessica Freedman.

"Forty!" shouted a little girl in a checked western shirt.

52

"*One!*" screamed Kate. "After that, the jail isn't empty anymore!"

I honked my bike horn and howled, and all the kids giggled.

"What do you call an outlaw with a cold?" Kate asked then.

"Let's see. . . ," I said thoughtfully. "What about . . . a *sick*-shooter?"

More giggling.

"What is a colt after it's one year old?" said Kate.

"A horse!" shouted David Reese, one of the Reese twins.

"No — *two years old*!" I yelled. "Want to hear a dirty joke?"

"Sure!" said Kate.

"*The cowboy fell in the mudhole!*"

Kate and I squawked and tooted and turned some cartwheels. We heard Jessica say to Danny Reese, the other twin, "I think it's a different Sparkly. This one's a lot shorter, but I like her even better!"

Kate looked sort of pleased, but all she said to me was, "Does Stephanie realize she's being paid to tape the party, not to talk?" Stephanie *was* taping, but Christy was also talking her ear off.

"I always knew what looked right on me," Christy was saying, "even when I was little. I remember when I was around three years old. . . ."

"Oh, no — the story of her life!" Kate moaned.

"My mom was getting me dressed for a party," Christy continued. "She wanted me to wear a yellow dress! Can you imagine — with my coloring?" Christy has kind of golden–brown hair and olive skin. I could see her point.

Stephanie nodded sympathetically and stopped the camera to talk to her. "Yeah, I know. My mother used to dress me in light blue all the time, and light blue doesn't do a thing for me . . ."

". . . so apparently I had a real temper tantrum, because there was no way I was going to wear yellow, even at that age . . ."

"LIGHTS, CAMERA, ACTION!" Kate thundered.

Stephanie jumped a mile, and whipped the video camera back up to her eye.

Kate and I told some more jokes, and then Jeffrey opened his presents. He got guns and holsters, a plastic ranch set, and a rubber rattlesnake. His favorite gift was from his grandparents, a complete cowboy outfit, down to the boots and spurs.

"He's obviously into clothes, like his sister," Kate murmured.

Then Mrs. Soames lit the candles, and we all

sang "Happy Birthday" as Jeffrey blew them out. The cake was cut, and the kids ate enough for an army. After that, Kate and I joined in a couple of the games: musical chairs, and pin the tail on the bucking bronco.

By five o'clock when Dr. Beekman picked us up, we were totally worn out. But we'd made thirty-five dollars, and the kids had had a great time.

I think Kate had enjoyed herself, too, but she would never admit it. She was still annoyed with Stephanie, and Stephanie wasn't very pleased with Kate, either. The car ride back home was as silent as the one *to* the Soameses' had been.

"Are we going to practice tomorrow with Adelaide?" I finally said.

"I can't," said Stephanie. "I'm busy. We'll have to wait until Monday."

After we dropped Stephanie off, Kate exclaimed, "See what I mean? If she really has a sprained ankle, how can she be busy?"

We found out on Sunday afternoon, when Kate and I got together to work on the poster for Patti's entry in the science fair.

On a big piece of white cardboard, we lined off ten rectangles. At the top, in block letters, Kate printed THE TRUTH ABOUT CATS. She's a thousand times

55

neater at writing than I am. Then, in each of the rectangles, we wrote one of the facts Patti had given us: "Cats need nineteen hours of sleep a day," and "Cats use their whiskers as feelers."

We borrowed my dad's Polaroid to take photographs of Rocky to illustrate each fact, and added the photos to the rectangles. In the last rectangle, Kate printed, "Are cats intelligent?" We didn't need a photograph for that one, because we'd have Adelaide in the flesh — trained and ready for action.

We fiddled with the poster for three or four hours. When we'd finished, we decided to groom Bullwinkle, because he was shedding black hair all over the house. Kate and I were standing in the driveway, brushing him, when a car honked at us as it drove by. BORN TO SHOP, the bumper sticker said.

"That's Christy Soames and her mom!" I exclaimed over Bullwinkle's barks.

"Right," said Kate, staring up Pine Street after them. "And they're stopping at Stephanie's house."

I planned to call Stephanie that evening to try to find out what was going on with her and Christy. But Roger stayed on the phone with Linda half the night, so I didn't get the chance to.

Because of her ankle, Stephanie didn't ride to school with us on Monday. We didn't have a chance to talk about anything at lunch, either. No sooner had the three of us sat down at our table, than Christy Soames sat down, too!

"Hi, there!" she screeched. "We had such a great time yesterday, didn't we, Steffi?"

"*Steffi?*" Kate repeated, raising an eyebrow.

"That's right, we had a *great* time," Stephanie said, glaring at Kate.

"We looked at some of my fashion magazines, and Steffi showed me how to braid my hair in a French braid" — Christy does have nice hair, thick and wavy — "and she told me about this girl she knows back in the city who's a model. That's what I want to do, become a fashion model. I think I've got the looks for it, don't you?"

"I think she's got the brains for it," Kate whispered.

Christy didn't hear Kate, because she was still blabbing on about herself. "I'm tall enough, and I'm just naturally thin, and — "

"I have to go to the library," Kate said, interrupting the stream of words. She picked up her tray. "Lauren, are you coming?"

Did I see Stephanie barely shake her head at me? But I was as bored with Christy as Kate was. "Sure. I have something to look up, too. Stephanie, what about this afternoon? You know — Adelaide?"

"Why don't you ride over to my house around four?" Stephanie said.

"Okay," I said, and Kate nodded.

"Great," said Stephanie, and Christy started talking again.

Chapter 7

A postcard came from Patti that day. Stephanie showed it to us as soon as we got to her house after school. On the front of the card there was a picture of an airport. On the back Patti had written: "I miss you guys already. Give Adelaide a big hug for me. Love, Patti."

"Patti is great," Kate said sadly. "Nice, serious, smart, not at all self-centered. . . ." She raised an eyebrow at Stephanie.

Stephanie's cheeks turned an angry red. "Listen, Kate — if you have any problems with Christy . . ."

"How's your ankle, Stephanie?" I sputtered. It was the first thing that popped into my mind that might head her off.

"Better. Thanks for asking, Lauren," Stephanie replied, looking down at her left foot.

"You've taken the bandage off?" I asked.

"Yeah, it started to itch," Stephanie said. She waved her foot at us, as if to tell us, "This'll show you I didn't make it up!"

Her ankle wasn't very swollen, but it was definitely bruised. There were black-and-blue blotches all around the joint on the outside of her foot. I looked at Kate. She'd been wrong after all.

We had been without Patti for only a few days so far, and already the Sleepover Friends had problems. This whole thing had started because Kate had been nervous about being a clown — it wasn't really her kind of thing. So she blamed Stephanie for forcing her into it by deciding the sprain was faked. It was true that Stephanie *could* have faked it, because she doesn't like to look silly any more than Kate does.

Stephanie, meanwhile, got mad because Kate hadn't believed her, so she decided to annoy Kate with Christy. I didn't think Stephanie was so wild about Christy herself, but she wasn't going to admit it. Stephanie would probably go on annoying Kate until Kate apologized, which Kate was too stubborn to do. After a while, they'd both get over it. They always did.

Unless Stephanie actually *liked* Christy, in which case the Sleepover Friends were *really* in a mess!

Patti, you can't move to Alaska! I thought to myself, hoping Patti was receiving my brain waves somehow. We need you right here! Please come back soon!

Stephanie had set up a card table in the living room. "To make the science fair practice as much like the real thing as possible," she said. There was also a container of "food bribes" for Adelaide: bits of ham and cheese, and some anchovy paste.

Right away, though, Stephanie and Kate disagreed on how to go about the practice. Stephanie brought Adelaide out of the bedroom and set her down on the card table. Adelaide immediately dozed off.

"Wake up, sweetie," said Stephanie, waving the container of food under the kitten's nose. When Adelaide opened her eyes, Stephanie gave her a piece of ham.

"Don't feed her until she's done some tricks," Kate directed.

"A little bite won't hurt," Stephanie said briskly. "Up, Adelaide."

Adelaide raised up on her hind legs.

61

"See?" Stephanie said, giving Adelaide another piece of ham.

Kate shook her head and frowned. "But she'll do it without the food," Kate argued. "Adelaide, roll over."

The kitten rolled over three times on the card table.

"See?" Kate said smugly.

"Adelaide — jump!" said Stephanie, holding out her arms. The kitten leaped into Stephanie's arms. Stephanie set her down on the table again, and fed her a piece of cheese.

"I think it might look better if she jumped into a box, or a basket," said Kate. "Like this one."

Kate dumped the magazines out of a straw basket at the end of the Greens' couch, set a small pillow in it, and held it close to her body. "Adelaide — jump!" Kate ordered.

Adelaide sailed neatly into the basket. Kate gave the kitten a pat and put her back on the table.

"I don't know . . ." said Stephanie. "It looks a little too much like basketball to me. I think the arms are better after all. Jump, Adelaide."

The kitten gazed uneasily around the room, instead of focusing on Stephanie.

"The two of you are going to drive her crazy,"

I warned. "You'd better leave her alone for a while."

"She's fine," Stephanie said, offering Adelaide a dab of anchovy paste. When she had gotten the kitten's attention, Stephanie ordered, "Come on, Adelaide — jump!"

Adelaide jumped, all right, but she'd had enough of Stephanie and Kate's practice session. She landed in Stephanie's arms and kept right on going, up over Stephanie's shoulder and down to the floor. Before anyone could grab her, Adelaide had scooted through the living-room door and out into the hall.

"Now you've done it!" Kate said to Stephanie as we raced after the kitten. "Why are you so stubborn?"

"Me, stubborn?" said Stephanie. "Hah!"

"Now you've *both* done it!" I yelled. "What if we've lost Patti's kitten?"

There wasn't much chance of Adelaide getting outside, as long as we didn't open any windows or doors. But the Greens' house is large, and there are hundreds of places a half-grown kitten could hide.

"I'll try the kitchen," Kate said.

"I'll take the dining room," I said.

And Stephanie searched the bedrooms, starting with her parents'.

63

We went through the entire house — closets, cabinets, and all with no luck.

"Now what?" said Kate anxiously.

"Let's look again," said Stephanie, pretty worried herself. "This time we'll go through one room at a time, together."

We searched in things, under things, and through things for what seemed like hours. I don't think we would have ever found Adelaide if it hadn't been for Cinders.

He finally woke up from his afternoon nap on Stephanie's bed and walked straight over to her bookcase. Cinders stuck a paw between the back of the bookcase and the wall, and meowed loudly.

"What have you got back there, Cinders?" Stephanie said, peering into the crack.

And there was Adelaide, scrunched into a space about as wide as two thick magazines.

"Adelaide!" Stephanie shrieked, dragging her out and smoothing down her ruffled fur. "Thank goodness!"

Stephanie set the kitten down on her rug and Adelaide promptly threw up.

"I *told* you it was too much food," said Kate, having the last word.

Chapter
8

I think there was a silent agreement between Kate and Stephanie not to practice with Adelaide any more and ruin Patti's good work.

The Riverhurst Elementary School Science Fair was held in the gym on Wednesday, right after school. Mrs. Green would be driving Adelaide over in Cinders's big cat-carrier, along with the card table. My mom was dropping off the poster Kate and I had made.

The gym was a madhouse, with about fifty or sixty kids setting up all kinds of exhibits. There was a lot of noise: whirs, squeaks, hums, and squeals. Three sixth-graders had put together a robot out of garbage — tin cans, metal ice-cube trays, parts of cars, and an old telephone — that kept acting up and crashing into things.

"Let's get as far away from that gizmo as we can," said Stephanie. "I don't think Adelaide would like it too much."

Todd Farrell, a really nice guy from 5A, had made an electric fan that ran on natural current from an Idaho potato — I'm not kidding! And Walter Williams, a little fourth-grader who lives in the house behind the Greens', had designed an incredible solar-powered model airplane from scratch. He'll probably be a famous scientist one day, and I'll be sorry I wasn't nicer to him when he had a big crush on me.

"Stephanie!" Mrs. Green walked through the double doors at the end of the gym with the carrier. My mom was behind her, our poster in one hand, the card table in the other. We ran to help them.

"Impressive!" Mom said, looking around at some of the entries.

"There was a lot more scientific stuff to Patti's exhibit, too, like information about a cat's brain waves, and their sleep-wake patterns," Kate told her, "but we'll just have to do the best we can without it."

"I'm sure Patti will be thrilled that you went to all this trouble for her," my mother said.

We set down our stuff in a quiet corner. We were setting up the card table when who should stroll by but Wayne Miller!

"This isn't a pet show, it's a science fair!" Wayne said, frowning at Adelaide in the carrier. "Dumb cat!"

"Stick around," Stephanie told him. "If you think cats are dumb, you may learn something . . . if it's possible."

Wayne made a rude noise. "So where's the fourth one?" he asked me.

"If you mean Patti, she's in Alaska for a week," I replied.

Wayne snickered. "Boy, did she go to a lot of trouble to get out of the Bike-a-thon — Alaska!" He shook his head and looked superior. "I knew you'd never do it, anyway. Twenty miles is way too much for a *girl*."

The way Wayne Miller says *girl* drives me crazy! "Oh, yeah?" I said. "Not this *girl*. For your information, *I'm* still in the Bike-a-thon. Just be sure you don't slow down, or I'll roll right over you!"

Wayne burst out laughing. "You're real funny, Lauren!" he said as he swaggered off.

"Yech!" I said through clenched teeth. "He makes me sick!"

"Now you'll *have* to ride in the Bike-a-thon," Kate said. "And twenty miles is quite a stretch without company."

"I'll be fine," I said grimly.

A bell rang, to let us know that the science-fair judges would be making their rounds soon. There were three of them: Mr. Helms, a sixth-grade teacher; Mrs. Milton, the teacher in 5A; and Mr. Keeler, who teaches fourth grade. Mrs. Milton is very strict, but Mr. Keeler is okay. Kate had him last year.

They made their way slowly around the gym, looking carefully at each of the exhibits, asking questions, writing in their notebooks. We could tell they were really knocked out by Walter Williams' airplane, but the kid *is* a genius, after all.

"What have we got here?" Mr. Keeler said when they stopped at our table. "I don't see your name on our list, Kate."

"Actually, it's Patti Jenkins's entry, Mr. Keeler," Kate explained. "She's away for a week, and we thought we'd enter for her. Patti was very upset about having to miss the fair."

"Hmmm." Mrs. Milton was checking our poster. "Interesting, but I'm not sure that it's strictly scientific. . . ."

"The most interesting part of Patti's project is the work she did with her kitten," Stephanie said quickly. She opened the carrier and lifted out Adelaide.

"That's right," Kate added. "Patti set out to prove that cats do have intelligence — that they are trainable."

Stephanie put Adelaide down on the card table. The kitten gazed calmly around the noisy gym, then stared up at the judges.

"Isn't she pretty!" said Mrs. Milton. "I have a cat myself, but I'll have to admit, he can't do anything except turn over his food dish."

"Cats can learn if they're taught early enough in their lives," Stephanie said, "and I think Patti has proved this with Adelaide." She tapped the kitten on the head. "Ready, Adelaide? *Up!*"

Stephanie put Adelaide through all of her tricks, and the black-and-white kitten performed them like a pro. Sitting up, rolling over, jumping — Adelaide didn't hesitate, or make a single mistake.

The judges all clapped for Adelaide's performance and told us how much they'd enjoyed it. Then they scribbled in their notebooks and moved on.

When they had finished examining every one of

69

the entries, Mr. Keeler, Mrs. Milton, and Mr. Helms huddled together at the end of the gym and talked things over.

"There are four kinds of ribbons," Stephanie said. "Walter told me. Blue for first, red for second, yellow for third, and green for honorable mention. And there are several different categories. I'm sure we'll win something in one of them."

"You mean, Patti will," Kate said.

"Right," Stephanie agreed.

Finally, they seemed to have made up their minds. Mrs. Milton took a handful of ribbons out of her shoulder bag, and the judges stepped forward.

Walter Williams was one of the first kids to get a blue ribbon. A photographer from the Riverhurst newspaper snapped his photo, while Walter held the solar plane toward the camera and grinned away, his red hair sticking straight up in back. Another blue ribbon went to Pete Stone, from 5B, for his experiment with heredity in hamsters. He had mated two brown males with two white females. When they had babies, he made a chart to show what colors they were and how many were each color. So far, there were twenty babies. Next to Pete's display was a big sign that said, FREE!!! TO GOOD HOMES.

A third-grader won a yellow ribbon for her exhibit of the major food groups. She had made a huge collage, and just thinking about cutting that many tiny bananas and beans out of magazines made my fingers ache. The three guys with their garbage robot were about to get a blue ribbon, but their entry got away from them again and ran over Mrs. Milton's feet. They ended up with a red ribbon instead. So did Todd Farrell, for his potato fan.

We got a red ribbon, too! After Mrs. Milton said what she did about our exhibit not being very scientific, I thought we might end up with an honorable mention, if we won anything at all.

"We were lucky Mrs. Milton likes cats," Kate whispered. Mr. Helms handed Stephanie a large, shiny, red ribbon with "Riverhurst Elementary School Science Fair — Second Place — General" printed on it in gold. Mrs. Milton gave Adelaide a final pat before she followed the other two teachers on to the next entry.

When the news photographers took our picture with Adelaide, we told him to make sure to give all the credit to Patti Jenkins from 5B.

"She's going to die when she sees her name in the paper!" Stephanie exclaimed.

"And Adelaide's picture," Kate added. "Great work, guys!"

It *had* been great, especially since Kate and Stephanie were getting along instead of bickering. Too bad it didn't last. . . .

Chapter
9

Everything blew up again after school on Friday. Stephanie was back on her bike for the first time since she'd sprained her ankle. She and Kate and I were pedaling home. We'd glided to a stop at the corner of South Road and Pine Street before splitting up until the sleepover at Kate's that night.

"I think Dad's going to take us out for Chinese food," Kate said. "Then, on channel K, there's a double-feature of new monster movies from Japan. . . ."

Stephanie cleared her throat. "Kate," she said firmly, "there's someone I'd like to bring to the sleepover tonight. . . ."

Christy? I groaned to myself.

Kate was thinking the same thing, only she didn't

73

keep it to herself — she exploded! *"Christy Soames? Stephanie, we've sat through enough boring lunches with that girl this week to last a lifetime! How can you be friends with someone so shallow?"*

"Are you trying to tell me who to be friends with, Kate Beekman?" Stephanie was practically shouting, and her cheeks were beet-red.

"I can't believe you'd have the nerve to force her on Lauren and me — in my own house!" Kate went on, not listening to Stephanie at all.

Suddenly, I couldn't take one more second of it! "I can't stand this!" I bellowed. "I don't want to know either of you, until both of you have apologized to each other!"

I pedaled off in the direction of my house, slinging gravel with my back tire. But not before I heard Kate yell, "Apologize for *what*?"

Stephanie screeched, "You think you're so smart, Kate Beekman! I wasn't talking about inviting Christy Soames at all. I was talking about inviting Jane Skyes!" Jane is a really nice girl in our room who had a giant sleepover for the whole class a few months back.

Then both of them screamed at my back, "You always take *her* side!"

I turned into our driveway, put my bike in the

74

garage, and stamped up the steps into the kitchen, slamming the door closed behind me.

"Lauren, is that you?" my mom called from upstairs.

"Yeah, Mom. And I'm going to be home tonight. Bullwinkle, get your tongue off my head!" Bullwinkle was leaning on the hall table and licking my face.

My mother stared down at me over the banister. "No sleepover at Kate's?"

"No." For the first time in I don't know how long, no Friday-night sleepover at all.

So what? I said to myself. I couldn't have stayed up late anyway, because of the Bike-a-thon. I'll get a lot of sleep, and be in much better shape tomorrow than I would've been if I'd watched monster movies all night long and crammed myself full of junk food.

But it wasn't much comfort. I didn't call Kate or Stephanie that evening, and they didn't call me. I was sure they were as angry at me as I was at them.

I woke up early the next morning — Bullwinkle had crawled into bed with me. Dad was already downstairs, making one of his special Saturday breakfasts.

"Fresh blueberry muffins, sausages, scrambled eggs," he announced. "Eat up. You'll need lots of carbohydrates for the Bike-a-thon."

But I felt too rotten to eat very much. When I stepped outside and looked up at the sky, I felt even worse: Big gray clouds covered most of it, with blacker clouds near the edges.

I could have pulled out of the race, of course, but I didn't want to have to listen to Wayne Miller for the rest of my life. Besides, I was afraid Patti would feel bad if she thought I had dropped out because of her.

By the time I'd ridden to the take-off point at the courthouse, it was beginning to drizzle. I was wearing my blue plastic poncho, but rain was dripping off my hood, onto my face, and down my neck. It cheered me up to see Wayne Miller looking pretty unhappy, too, in his rubber raincoat. His pal, Ronny Wallace, looked even worse. He was wearing a short windbreaker, and everything it didn't cover up was getting slowly soaked.

There was a huge crowd of bikers on the lawn, determined to have a good time at the Bike-a-thon in spite of the crummy weather.

When the starting gun went off, I lost sight of Wayne and Ronny. There were so many participants that I couldn't tell whether I pulled onto the road in front of Wayne, or behind him.

Riverhurst is kind of hilly in spots. I was pedaling

hard to get to the top of the hill behind Riverhurst Hospital when someone in the crowd called out, "Hey, wait up!"

I figured it couldn't have anything to do with me, so I didn't turn around until I heard Kate's voice coming up. "Lauren — slow down!"

I almost fell off my bike! It was Kate and Stephanie, not the most enthusiastic athletes under normal conditions, pedaling up a steep hill in the rain!

"What are you doing here?" I gasped, pulling off the road onto the shoulder.

"Oh, I thought I needed some curl in my hair," Stephanie said wryly. Her hair absolutely frizzes if there's the slightest bit of moisture in the air.

"We thought we'd keep you company," Kate said. "Twenty miles is an awfully long way to ride by yourself."

"So did you guys . . . uh . . ." I fumbled.

"Yes, we apologized to each other," Stephanie said. "And we apologize to you, too."

"We were acting like babies," Kate admitted, "because we were upset about what might happen with Patti."

After she said "Patti," the three of us were quiet for a moment, really missing her.

"Let's get moving, before we drown out here,"

Stephanie said, and we started up the hill together.

We hadn't ridden far when Kate asked, "What is that noise? Is there something wrong with your chain, Lauren?"

"It's my stomach growling," I admitted sheepishly. Since everything was okay with us again, my appetite was coming back like crazy. "I didn't eat much breakfast, so I'm starving," I told Kate and Stephanie.

"No problem," said Stephanie. "Let's pull into that bus stop up ahead to get out of the rain."

"What about the race?" I protested.

"The most important thing is finishing, right?" Kate said. "We'll finish."

"Besides, don't you remember the tortoise and the hare?" said Stephanie.

We leaned our bikes against the back of the three-sided bus-stop shed, and sat down on the wooden bench. Stephanie pulled off her red poncho. Underneath it was her backpack, which was absolutely stuffed.

"Hot chocolate, anybody?" she said, taking a thermos and three plastic cups out of the largest compartment. She unzipped a side pocket. "Doughnuts? Croissants? Bagels?"

Kate burst out laughing. "You're like the old

78

fisherman's wife who had a pot of soup that was never empty. What else have you got there?"

Stephanie unzipped a second side pocket. "Napkins. And some candy bars, for quick energy."

We needed a lot of energy just to get through half that food. By the time we'd finished eating, the sky was starting to clear.

"That was terrific," I said as we climbed back on our bikes. "The only thing I regret is, that jerk Wayne will probably beat us to the finish line by two hours."

"Slow and steady," Stephanie reminded me.

She and Kate did pretty well for the first ten miles or so. Then they started to lag.

"My legs are beginning to feel like lead weights," Kate puffed as we pedaled up the hill, just before you get to the vegetable stand at Briermere Farm.

"Mine are on *fire*!" Stephanie groaned. "And I'm *sweaty*!" Her face was bright red, and her hair was completely frizzed out. "I think we're going to have to stop for a second. . . ."

Stephanie veered onto the farm lawn. Then she sort of fell off her bike onto the damp grass. "Water . . . water . . . ," she croaked.

"How about a soda?" I suggested. There's a machine on the front porch of the stand.

"I can't move . . . ," Stephanie whispered, her eyes closed.

"I can't, either." Kate was rubbing her calves with a pained expression on her face.

"I'll get them," I said. My legs felt fine, probably because of all the exercising Patti and I had done. I was a little worried about Kate and Stephanie, though.

They perked up a bit after they'd each drunk a soda. "There aren't any hills for a couple of miles," I told them. "Ready to go on?"

"Might as well," Kate said grimly, climbing onto her bike and wobbling up the road.

"Coming." Stephanie staggered to her feet, groaned loudly as she sat down on her bike again, and pedaled slowly after Kate.

If they were in such bad shape already, and there were at least eight more miles to finish the course . . . "Listen, if you guys want to stop, the Race Committee is sending a van around to pick up people who drop out . . . ," I said.

"We're not dead yet!" Kate said firmly, but she made a face every time she pushed down on a pedal.

I don't know how long Kate and Stephanie would have stuck it out if we hadn't rounded the curve past Tully's Fish Market and seen Ronny Wallace. He was sitting next to his bike at the side of the road, his broken bike-chain in his hand. He was drenched, too.

Kate started pedaling like crazy. "I think I just found my second wind," she said.

Even Stephanie sat up straight and stopped groaning.

"Hi-i-i-i-i!" we all yelled cheerfully as we coasted past.

"One down, one to go," said Kate.

"I wonder where Wayne is," I said.

I didn't have to wonder long.

When you pass the mall, the road makes a big circle around Munn's Pond and the Riverhurst Wildlife Refuge. There's a little parking space at the top of a hill, where people stop for a scenic view. Kate and Stephanie and I were resting there for a second, getting our wind back, when suddenly Stephanie squawked, "There he goes!" She was pointing to one of the brushier parts of the Refuge.

"Who?" Kate and I asked.

"Wayne! See his yellow slicker?"

Wayne Miller was trying to make sure he'd beat me. He'd left the road, and was pushing his bike through the Refuge!

"That'll cut several miles off the route," Kate

said. "What a cheater!" She leaped onto her bike and tore down the road.

"We can still catch up with him if we hustle," I said, jumping onto my bike, too.

"The only way I can keep going is by telling myself I'll lose ten pounds, at least!" Stephanie moaned. But she pedaled bravely on.

Luckily, from that point on, most of the course was downhill. We raced around the circle, and sped down Roanoke Drive, with Stephanie groaning at every bump.

"Do you see Wayne anywhere?" I asked Kate.

Kate shook her head. "He must be ahead of us," she said.

The last five or six blocks of the Bike-a-thon route were lined with cheering people. I spotted my mom and dad, Mr. Green with the video camera, and Dr. Beekman wearing his hospital whites.

As we streaked across the finish line — at least, Kate and I streaked; Stephanie struggled, to put it politely — I thought I'd caught sight of someone else familiar out of the corner of my eye. But it couldn't have been . . . it *was*!

"Patti!" I hollered.

Kate and Stephanie and I dropped our bikes. The

four of us threw our arms around each other and jumped up and down and screamed!

When we'd calmed down enough to talk, Stephanie asked, "What are you doing here? Weren't you supposed to come back on Tuesday?"

Patti was beaming. "WE'RE NOT MOVING!" she shouted. I didn't even know she could get that loud.

"*Not moving?*" "What happened?" "Did you talk your parents out of it?" We all began speaking at once. That last question was from Stephanie.

"It was partly that, and partly the dirty air — "

"Dirty air? In Alaska?" I was shocked!

" — and partly that the university in Riverhurst called up my parents and offered big promotions and more money!" Patti finished.

"Oh, no!" Stephanie said.

"Stephanie, what's wrong with you?" Kate asked. "That's fantastic news."

"No, no! That's not it!" Stephanie was laughing so hard she could hardly speak, so she pointed back toward the Bike-a-thon route.

It was then that Wayne Miller rolled over the finish line. Not rolled, exactly — flumped over the finish line on two flat tires is more like it.

Wayne wasn't in much better shape than his bike. His face was scratched, his slicker ripped, and his complexion was a little green. He looked even sicker when he saw us.

"Wayne Miller! You let yourself get beaten by mere girls?" Kate said sternly.

"Never would have happened if my stupid bike hadn't broken down," Wayne mumbled.

"A trail bike might've worked better where you were going," I said helpfully. "Or maybe a tank. . . ."

Stephanie shook her head. "Cheaters never wi-in, cheaters never wi-in," she sang softly.

"Dumb girls!" But Wayne sounded a lot less positive than usual. Pushing his beat-up bike, he skulked away.

"I feel like I've been gone forever," Patti said. "What did I miss at the sleepover last night?"

I glanced at Kate and Stephanie.

"We didn't have a sleepover last night," Kate said.

"It just wouldn't have been the same without you," said Stephanie.

"Then why don't we have one at my house tonight?" Patti suggested with a big smile. "I already asked Mom and Dad, and they said it was okay!"

"Sounds great to me," I said.

"Me, too," said Kate.

"I'll bring Adelaide when I come," Stephanie said.

"Maybe we should have another kitten sleep-over," said Patti.

"Cinders and Adelaide are getting along really well now," Stephanie reported.

"Rocky accepts the invitation," I said.

"Fredericka, too," said Kate.

Stephanie, Kate, and I picked our bikes up and walked with Patti to the rack where she'd left hers.

"I brought back some little surprises for you from Alaska," Patti said.

"We've got a surprise for you, too!" Kate told her.

Chapter 10

We didn't go over to Patti's until after dinner, because the Jenkinses were bound to be too tired to have to cook a meal. Mr. and Mrs. Jenkins were in the laundry room, washing the clothes they'd unpacked, when Kate and I got to the house.

"Hello, girls," they called down the hall.

"We're really glad you're staying," Kate called back.

"So are we!" said Mrs. Jenkins.

"Where's Horace?" I asked Patti.

"Spending the night with the Reese twins," she said. "We've got the whole house to ourselves."

We headed for the stairs. "All the snacks I could come up with are upstairs in my bedroom," Patti told us.

"Not for long," I said when she'd pushed open the door. Stephanie was lying on the floor next to the tray, already chowing down.

"I can't move, but I can eat. The Bike-a-thon," she said around a mouthful of dip-and-cracker, "did incredible things to my appetite." Her appetite isn't bad on normal days. I unwrapped Rocky and grabbed a cracker before everything disappeared.

"Yummy!" I said after I'd scooped up some dip. "What is it?"

"They made it at our hotel, and I asked for the recipe," Patti said. "Tuna, cream cheese, catsup, and some other stuff, mixed up in the blender."

Kate set Fredericka's box down to take some, too. "Patti's Alaska Dip," she named it after a taste. "It's great."

"So tell me everything," Patti said, sitting down next to Stephanie. "How was the party at the Soameses'?"

"I sprained my ankle just before it started," Stephanie said with an eye on Kate, "and Kate had to take my place as a clown. She was terrific."

"It was sort of fun, actually." Kate had finally admitted it.

"Oh . . . well, if you want to be Sparkly . . ." Patti began.

"No, no . . . I think once was enough," Kate said.

"Anything interesting happen at school this week?" Patti asked.

"As a matter of fact . . ." Stephanie unzipped a side pocket of her backpack. "This is for you. From Kate, Lauren, and me. And Adelaide." She handed Patti something wrapped in white tissue paper.

Patti unwrapped it carefully. "Oh, wow!" Tears came to her eyes as she read what was written on the ribbon. She looked at the three of us. "You guys are the best!"

"If you had been there, I'm sure it would've been a blue ribbon," I told her.

"I personally think red looks better on Adelaide," Stephanie said. She draped the ribbon across Patti's kitten, asleep on the desk chair.

"White and black and red — you would," Kate said, and we all giggled.

"And . . . ," Stephanie said, reaching into her backpack again with a dramatic flourish. "Adelaide's picture is in the paper," I finished, as Stephanie unfolded the article.

"Along with Walter Williams — he won a blue ribbon for his solar plane," Stephanie said. "So did Pete Stone, for an experiment with hamsters."

"And Todd Farrell got a red one, for his potato fan," said Kate.

"Good for Todd!" Patti said.

"Then on Friday, Lauren got mad at Stephanie and me," Kate teased.

"You did?" Patti said to me. "Why?"

"The minute you left, they started acting like babies," I said with a grin. "Kate was being bossy, and Stephanie started hanging around with Christy Soames. . . ."

"Hey, what's happening with Christy, anyway?" Kate asked Stephanie.

"Something snapped. I decided I couldn't stand to be called 'Steffi' one more time," Stephanie said.

Patti laughed. "You're definitely not a Steffi."

"And there's more to life than shopping," Stephanie added.

"All in all, it's a good thing you're back," I told Patti.

"And you'd better not leave again," Stephanie added.

Patti shook her head. "My parents are signing contracts for the next five years, at least." She stood up. "Now I'm going to show you your surprises."

She opened her suitcase and took out four small packages wrapped in brown paper. Each package had one of our first initials printed on it: L, K, S, and P.

"I got this one for you, Lauren, because it made me think of — " Patti began.

I'd ripped the brown paper off to find a beautiful little bear cub, carved out of a dark-gray-and-white stone. "Of Bullwinkle!" I finished for her. "I love it!"

Stephanie's was a plump little penguin. "I thought you'd like it because of the color scheme," Patti said.

"It's perfect!" said Stephanie.

Kate's was a fawn, asleep with its legs tucked underneath it.

"They're all darling!" Kate said. "Who made them?"

"The Eskimos carve them during the winter months," Patti said. She unwrapped the package in her lap and held it up for us all to see. "Dad bought this one for me."

The carving was of the same gray stone, but it was larger, of four girls. They were standing in a circle, hugging one another, with big smiles on their faces.

"They remind me of us," Stephanie said.

Patti nodded. "My dad calls this 'The Sleepover Friends Forever.' "

"And we will be!" I said. Then Stephanie grabbed me and pulled me up, and I grabbed Kate, and Kate grabbed Patti, and we hugged one another in a real Sleepover Friends circle with big smiles on all of our Sleepover faces.

SLEEPOVER FRIENDS

#10 *Lauren's Sleepover Exchange*

The last two girls climbed down from the bus and glanced around for their hostesses. One was wearing jeans and Mercury jogging shoes, exactly like mine.

When we'd gotten closer, though, we saw that the girl in the jogging shoes was Kate's visitor, Darlene Kastner.

Darlene looked down at my feet in their Mercurys, and her fact lit up. "Am I staying with you?" she asked.

I shook my head. "No, Annette Hollis is." I was disappointed, because she looked like fun.

The last girl, who had to be Annette by process of elimination, was standing with her back to us. She didn't look even a little curious about finding her host.

I sighed. I had a feeling it was going to be a very long week.